TODAY IS THE DAY

For the Dawber family — E. W.
For Ellen Dumas, who celebrates everything — E. F.

Text copyright © 2015 by Eric Walters
Illustrations copyright © 2015 by Eugenie Fernandes

Published in Canada by Tundra Books, a division of Random House of Canada Limited,
a Penguin Random House Company.

Published in the United States by Tundra Books of Northern New York,
P.O. Box 1030, Plattsburgh, New York 12901

Library of Congress Control Number: 2013953673

**Library and Archives Canada Cataloguing in Publication**

Walters, Eric, 1957—, author
        Today is the day / by Eric Walters ; illustrated by Eugenie Fernandes.
Issued in print and electronic formats.

ISBN 978-1-77049-648-4 (bound).—ISBN 978-1-77049-650-7 (epub)
        I. Fernandes, Eugenie, 1943—, illustrator  II. Title.

PS8595.A598T63 2015          jC813'.54          C2014-906445-4
                                                 C2014-906446-2

Library of Congress Control Number: 2014951814

Edited by Debbie Rogosin and Samantha Swenson
Designed by Andrew Roberts
The artwork in this book was rendered in acrylic on paper.
The text was set in Zemke Hand.
Printed and bound in China

www.penguinrandomhouse.ca

1  2  3  4  5      20  19  18  17  16  15

# TODAY
## IS THE DAY

written by
## ERIC WALTERS

illustrated by
## EUGENIE FERNANDES

TUNDRA BOOKS

Mutanu's eyes popped open. She had been waiting for almost a year, and finally the day had arrived! She was so excited she wanted to shout, but she didn't want to wake the other girls.

She needn't have worried. Most of them had been awake so early *they* could have woken the roosters. They all knew that today was the day.

Mutanu's name meant 'happy.' Despite the death of her parents, and living with so little before she came to the orphanage, she always tried to be like her name. But on this morning, everybody was happy. The smiles were wider, the laughter louder and the voices brighter.

After breakfast, Mutanu and her friend Kanini tried to peek into the storage room. Behind the partly opened door were the usual bags of rice and maize and beans. But today there was more than just food.

Many of the children had lived at the orphanage for years, so they knew all about the wonderful things inside. For the newest children, like Mutanu and Kanini, this would be their first time. The other children had told them about the surprises in the storeroom, and they were excited to see for themselves.

$E$ven though today was the day, there were still chores to be done. Clothes needed to be washed, goats and chickens fed, wood chopped and crops picked. All the children helped in their own way.

Mutanu quickly finished sweeping the yard so she could do her favorite chore — feeding the orphanage dog. Her name was Rafiki, which meant 'friend' in Swahili.

The dog could sound fierce, but she was gentle with the children. Usually Rafiki went out at night to help the watchman guard the compound. Now she had another important job — she was the mother to a litter of puppies.

"Good morning, Rafiki," Mutanu said as she put down a bowl for the dog. Rafiki wagged her tail. The bowl was filled with porridge and table scraps, and at the bottom was a little piece of sausage Mutanu had saved from her breakfast. It was an extra-special meal for an extra-special day.

Mutanu picked up one of the puppies. "Rafiki, your babies were born on the twenty-first day of June. Now they are twenty-one days old."

Just then, Mutanu saw people arriving at the compound. That meant the time was getting closer! Mutanu's stomach fluttered with excitement. Gently she placed the puppy back beside Rafiki. "Take good care of your babies," she said, and she went to greet the people.

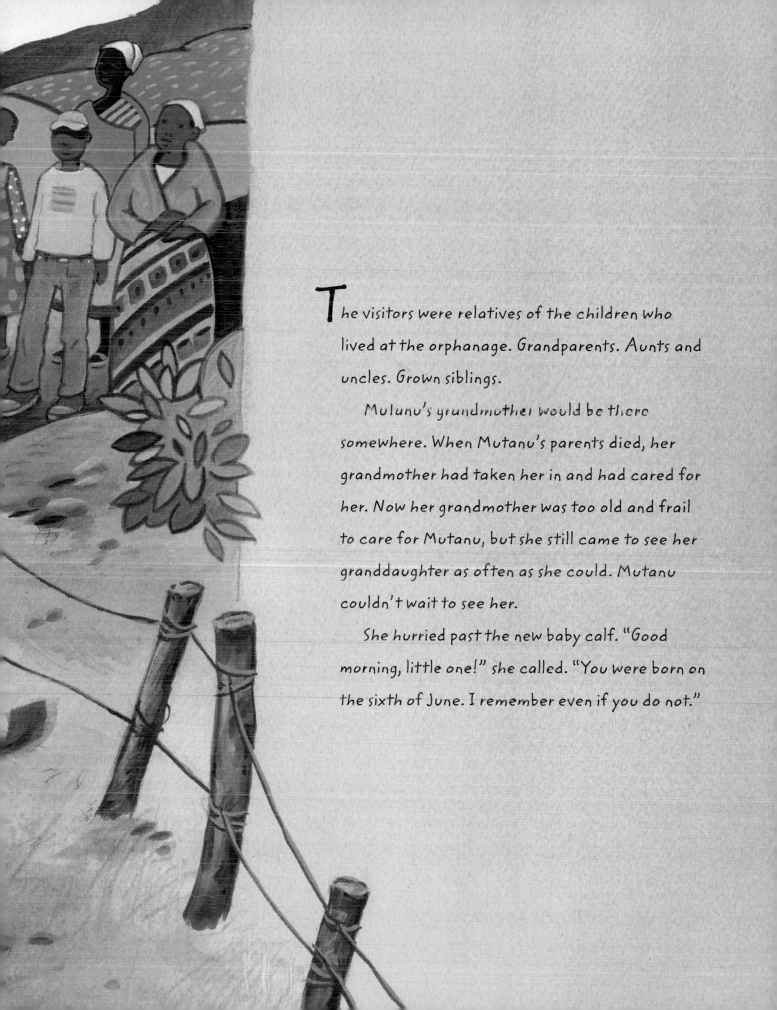

The visitors were relatives of the children who lived at the orphanage. Grandparents. Aunts and uncles. Grown siblings.

Mutanu's grandmother would be there somewhere. When Mutanu's parents died, her grandmother had taken her in and had cared for her. Now her grandmother was too old and frail to care for Mutanu, but she still came to see her granddaughter as often as she could. Mutanu couldn't wait to see her.

She hurried past the new baby calf. "Good morning, little one!" she called. "You were born on the sixth of June. I remember even if you do not."

She ran past the new baby goats and the chicks just out of their eggs. There were always new animal babies at the orphanage — chicks and calves, kittens and puppies, kids and lambs.

At last Mutanu found her grandmother!

"And how is my precious girl today?" her grandmother asked.

Mutanu wrapped her arms around her grandmother. "I could not be happier," she said.

They talked and talked until it was time for Mutanu to join the other children.

The matron welcomed the visitors. Greetings were offered, messages and news shared, and thanks given. The children shuffled and squirmed, too excited to stand still or listen.

Then it began. The moment all the children had been waiting for.

One by one, names were called and children came forward to get a cloth bag and a colorful hat. As they pulled things out of their bags, Mutanu saw toy cars and dolls, stuffed animals, shirts, balls and jump ropes, pencils, notebooks, toothbrushes and candy.

There were one hundred and fifteen children in all. Mutanu shifted from foot to foot, trying to be patient. But with each name that was called it became more difficult.

"Mutanu!" the matron finally called out. Mutanu jumped forward. The matron placed a hat on her head and a bag in her hand. It was heavy! Mutanu was eager to see the gifts in her bag — but they weren't what she *really* wanted. What she really wanted was still to come.

After all the children had received their gifts, they gathered in front of a large table that held fifteen cakes.

The matron held up her hand. When all was quiet, she spoke. "Each year we gather to celebrate the birthdays of all the children of the orphanage. Today is the day. Some of you know the date of your birth and some of you do not. For those who do not know, today and forever, July the twelfth will now officially be your birthday!"

Everyone clapped and cheered and hooted and laughed.

"Let us all sing!" the matron called out, and she began the song.

*This* was what Mutanu had been waiting for. She joined in, and her voice seemed louder and her smile brighter than all the others.

"Happy birthday to me,
Happy birthday to me,
Happy birthday, dear me,
Happy birthday to me!"

This day was about presents and cake and a shiny hat, but it was more than that for Mutanu.

Today, for the very first time, she knew that her coming into the world was not forgotten but was a cause for joyous celebration.

Today was more than just the day.

Today was Mutanu's day — her birthday!

# HAPPY BIRTHDAY TO ME!

The Creation of Hope (www.creationofhope.com) is located in Kikima, a rural community in Mbooni District, Kenya. It helps orphans throughout the region.

In this small community of less than 22,000 people, there are over 500 orphans. There are many reasons for this crisis. The main reason is HIV and AIDS. Other health concerns, accidents and abandonment are also factors. Children who have lost their parents are often taken in by relatives who may themselves be living in poverty. Or, as was the case for many of the children in our program, there was no one to care for them, and they were left to live on the streets and fend for themselves.

Kenya and Mbooni District

Mutanu and a puppy

Mutanu and the cow enclosure                    Younger girls' dormitory

Today, there are 55 children in our Rolling Hills residence. Over 50 others are given support to attend high school and to reside there. And more than 300 orphans and impoverished children are provided for so that they can live with extended family.

The births of many of the children born in rural Kenya are never registered. This could be because of poverty, illiteracy or even superstition, since some people believe that recording the birth of a child might be bad luck and result in that child's death. Sometimes the birth may be noted but not written down, and with the passage of time or the loss of parents, the date is forgotten.

A great number of the children in our program do not know the exact day of their birth. In some cases they don't even know the month or year. While it may seem like a common custom to give children special treatment on their birthdays, this is not the case for many orphans around the world. Their birthdays pass without recognition or acknowledgment and certainly without celebration.

Celebrating with loot bags

Kanini, which means 'little one' in Kikamba

Mueni giving the thumbs up

In places where there are so many orphans, their lives are often seen as having little value. People turn away, not out of cruelty but because resources are so few and the need is so great.

We wanted the children at our orphanage to see themselves as having value and to know that their births mattered. So we decided to hold a birthday party — a once-a-year celebration for all our children, whether they knew their date of birth or not. We wanted each child to have a birthday, and we wanted that day to be a joyous celebration!

Our first birthday party was held in 2011 for 54 orphans. In 2013, it grew to 115 orphans and 42 other children — a total of 157 children celebrating their birthdays together!

Each child at the party receives a loot bag. It is filled with gifts, including pens and pencils, school-books, stickers, a storybook, treats, a stuffed animal, socks, a T-shirt and sports equipment or a game. Each child also receives a balloon and a

Kay serving cake

Celebration

party hat, and some years there have been noisemakers, party masks and bubble makers.

And there is cake! Not just for the birthday celebrants, but for everybody — cousins, grandparents, aunts, uncles, guardians and visitors. These cakes are made by our staff in the oven in our residence — one of the few ovens in the entire district!

Cakes for all

Smiles from Mwau

Perhaps the most important gift, though, is what comes after. The staff works to ensure that each child receives a government-issued birth certificate that shows either the day that they know or believe is their birthday or the day that is decided upon as their birthday. With a birth certificate, the children are official. The government must acknowledge them as real people with all the rights of citizens.

Eric, Kilinda and Kilouzo proudly showing their birth certificates

Mutanu is one of the many orphans who now has a birthday and a birth certificate, and every year she looks forward to her birthday on July 12.

Happy birthday to the children of The Creation of Hope! Your birth is a cause for celebration!

**Eric Walters** Autumn 2015